Yes, all of that—and even more!
So what is Christmas really for?

The lights that glitter on the tree
Tell us Jesus came to be . . .

A light for us, and so we say,
"This Christmastime and every day,
Light our path, dear Lord, we pray."

Angels sparkling in the light
Remind us angels sang that night . . .

To sing to us, "Hooray! Hooray!
Good news! God's Son is born today!

Sing for joy on Christmas Day!”

The tree that's green when others die

Tells us Jesus came and why.

To give us life! And so we say,
"This Christmastime and every day,
Live in us, dear Lord, we pray."

Above our tree, the twinkling star
Tells us wise men traveled far . . .

To find the king, and so we say,

"This Christmastime and every day,
Be our king, dear Lord, we pray."

The gifts that sit beneath our tree

Tell us God loves you and me.

This Christmastime—and every day—